Praise for Storyshares

"One of the brightest innovators and game-changers in the education industry."
— Forbes

"Your success in applying research-validated practices to promote literacy serves as a valuable model for other organizations seeking to create evidence-based literacy programs."   — Library of Congress

"We need powerful social and educational innovation, and Storyshares is breaking new ground. The organization addresses critical problems facing our students and teachers. I am excited about the strategies it brings to the collective work of making sure every student has an equal chance in life."
— Teach For America

"It's the perfect idea. There's really nothing like this. I mean, wow, this will be a wonderful experience for young people."   — Andrea Davis Pinkney,
Executive Director, Scholastic

"Reading for meaning opens opportunities for a lifetime of learning. Providing emerging readers with engaging texts that are designed to offer both challenges and support for each individual will improve their lives for years to come. Storyshares is a wonderful start."

— David Rose, Co-founder of CAST & UDL

Erin and the Indian Bride

Storyshares presents

Published by Storyshares, LLC
Inspiring reading with a new kind of book.

Storyshares
Storyshares, LLC
24 N. Bryn Mawr Avenue #340
Bryn Mawr, Pennsylvania 19010-3304
www.storyshares.org

Interest Level: Middle School
Grade Level Equivalent: 3.5

ISBN 9781642615869
Book design by Saskia Globig

Erin and the Indian Bride

Javeria Kausar

Storyshares

Contents

1

"UGH!" I groan loudly and flop onto my bed.

My mother looks at me from across the room. She is busy folding clothes and arranging them neatly in a suitcase. I notice her roll her eyes.

I get up. Several boxes, tape rolls, markers, and sheets of bubble wrap are scattered around my bedroom floor. I carefully dodge them and make my way to a chair near my mom.

"UUGGGHHH!" I groan louder and collapse on the chair.

Mom rolls her eyes again. "What's wrong, Erin?"

"I seem to be unwell, Mom." I fake a cough. "Maybe I caught a cold." I close my eyes for extra effect.

"Really?" I can almost feel her cock an eyebrow. "You've caught a cold, have you?"

I nod weakly.

"In *summer*?" she asks.

I open my eyes nervously. "Uh, yes. It's so strange, isn't it? S-strange enough to cancel our trip and stay at home, right?"

I feel proud of my quick thinking. But Mom only crosses her arms and says, "I'd say it's strange enough to take you to the hospital."

At the sound of the word "hospital" I shoot up from the chair. *No! A doctor would instantly know that I'm perfectly fine.*

I finally stutter, "I'm fine, really. I'm fine, Mom."

"You better be. We have a flight to catch in forty-eight hours," Mom says chirpily.

I don't understand how she can be so cheerful at a time like this. I feel as though the world is about to collapse. I feel horrible. I feel homeless.

But of course, my mother would never understand that. I frown at the thought.

"Why don't you want to go to India, Erin?" She sounds concerned.

I bite my lip and remain quiet. It's not like she can understand.

She comes closer to me and whispers, "It'll be wonderful, honey." She squeezes my hand reassuringly.

I pull away but instantly regret doing so. In a low voice I say, "Do we really have to go?"

Somehow, my voice sounds more pained than I expected. My mother is taken aback too. After a year of joblessness, Dad had finally secured a job—but in a small city in *India*. As if to compensate for the bad offer, the company promised to provide accommodation for me and my mother in India.

My mother was as calm as ever. She immediately started packing. My father got busy with the paperwork. As for me, I struggled to stay calm and willed myself to believe that it was a dream that would end just as quickly as it started.

Only it didn't.

The gravity of the situation didn't hit me until my dad showed me the flight tickets this morning. My mind has been panicking ever since. Going to India means leaving London. It means a new house, a new school, and, worst of all, new people.

My mother puts her work aside and settles down on the floor. She is quiet, as though she's thinking of what to say. I want to tell her that I know what her answer's going to be: "Yes, we have to go, Erin."

I open my mouth to say something, but she speaks before I do.

"I'm sorry, Erin," she says slowly. She sighs. "I don't want to go to India any more than you do. I've lived in London all my life. I feel as though I'm leaving behind everything that is familiar."

My eyebrows shoot up in surprise. My mom—the pillar of the family, the sturdy mast of positivity, the bright ray of sunshine—is upset by this turn of events? I had never seen her complain about anything. I guess this move to India *is* a big deal. I'm relieved to know I'm not overreacting.

"I'm also worried about this change, Erin," she says softly. "But we have to stay strong or it will break your father's heart. All the arrangements have been made. There's no turning back. Besides, there's nothing left here. All we can do is calm down and prepare ourselves."

For the first time, I feel sorry for my mother. I openly show my disapproval whenever I want to, but Mom doesn't get to do that. She has to stay strong so Dad and I have someone to lean on for support.

I throw my arms around her and hug her tightly.

I'm amazed at the words that escape my lips. "We're gonna be fine, Mom."

My heart starts pounding. Just moments ago, I was telling myself the opposite. I was dreading the move to India because it means starting a new life. Because of my unnatural shyness and fear of people, it had taken me almost all of my twelve years to make a friend. How much longer would it take to adjust to a new country, a new culture, and turn a stranger into a friend?

I bury my face in my mother's shoulder and weep softly.

2

We enter the Vijayawada airport at eight in the morning. The entire journey lasted a little over 24 hours. We had to switch planes twice. It would be an understatement to say that my legs feel cramped.

"Dad, is it okay if I walk around a bit?"

"Sure, honey. Go take a look around. There are a lot of people here, so it'll be a while before we get to the immigration counter. I'll give you a call when we're close."

I nod and wander off. But there's not far to go. The airport is quite small, especially compared to the other airports I'd seen in London,

Delhi, and Hyderabad. It's not impressive in terms of style, but it is charming. It is spotlessly clean. The furniture is simple. There are hand-painted scenes on the walls—scenes of villagers and farmers with their families and houses.

I can't help but frown. The walls seem to be glaring at me, reminding me that I'm far away from home. For the first time, I notice the different people. I've seen Indians in my school, but I've never seen so many in one place—a place where I don't belong.

The sun pours in through the glass walls. I know it's the same sun, but it feels different. The air, the sun, and the plants are all foreign. Can this foreign land ever feel like home?

My phone vibrates in my pocket. It's Dad. I take a deep breath and walk back to my family—the only home I still have.

3

When we finally walk out with our luggage, we see a man holding a placard with the name *Eric Vainwright*.

My father whispers, "This is it," and puts on a smile.

He then waves at the man with the placard and approaches him. My mom and I quietly follow.

We are led to a big car. The man hauls our luggage over the car and secures it with ropes.

Dad turns to us and says, "His name is Suresh. He was sent by the company to pick us up. He'll be taking us to our new home."

We file into the car after Suresh is done loading our bags. Once he secures his seat belt, he turns back and offers us a big, toothy smile. "Welcome to India!"

I can feel the excitement in his voice.

"Thank you," Mom says. She elbows me.

I stop staring at his teeth, which are as dark as his skin, and muster a smile. "Thank you, sir."

He waves his hands frantically in front of me, "No, no, no, baby."

"Baby?" I'm shocked. "Why are you calling me that?"

"Why? Baby means child, no? You are a child, no?"

My father giggles. My face flushes red.

"Oh, it's habit," Suresh continues. "Here, we call kids 'baby' and kids call adults 'uncle' or 'auntie.' So don't call me 'sir.' Call me 'uncle,' please, baby."

"Only if you stop calling me 'baby,'" I say coldly.

My father loudly clears his throat, which translates to, "Mind your manners, young lady!"

Suresh seems hurt, but he tries to maintain his smile. "If I don't call you 'baby,' what I will call you?"

I bite my lip. I examine Suresh's graying hair and the many wrinkles that surround his eyes. He must be in his fifties already. He's just a grandpa who means well. I feel bad for behaving coldly.

"Just call me Erin," I mutter.

"Shall I call you 'madam'?" he asks brightly.

"No, no. Call me by my name," I say.

"What is your name then, little girl?"

"Erin."

"Eric? But that is your father's name, no?" He seems confused.

My father laughs and explains the difference between our names. Suresh laughs, apologizes, and starts the car.

Suresh keeps talking. It's as though he does not even pause for breath. Although he talks in English, I feel like I can't understand anything. My ears reject his excited voice. I tune it out.

My head is filled with thoughts of London. I always sat beside my dad when he drove. When we had free time, we would all sit in the car and I'd tell my dad where to go. I knew all the best places in the city. Car trips were the best.

I look out the window. I'm robbed of the one thing that gave me the most joy. The car trips required that I knew where I was going. But now I feel lost. I know nothing about this place.

4

The drive is longer than I expected. I have nothing to do except stare out the window. Unfamiliar trees and fields lay on both sides of the road. Cows, buffaloes, and white birds dot the scene. We pass a huge herd of goats and a couple of shepherds along the way. The smell of manure hits me, and I roll up the window.

It is nearly ten in the morning when we enter a town. I can see busy stalls and carts and tiny restaurants. Shops are crammed together like bricks in a wall. Fruit, vegetable, and flower vendors carry their goods in woven baskets. I can hear vendors crying at the top of their lungs to attract customers. We can hear them even through the rolled-up car windows.

Suresh asks if we would like some tea, and my parents get excited. Back home, we loved tea time. We had tea at least twice a day. I usually only had the cakes and biscuits, but I knew that tea helped my parents relax.

"Tea would be wonderful right now, Suresh," Dad says.

"Excellent! There's a stall here that sells the best tea in the world—no, no, in the universe! I'll take you there. I'm sure you'll love it," Suresh says.

After five minutes, the car halts by a footpath. Dad is about to open the door when Suresh stops him. "No, sir. You wait here. I'll get the tea."

We are all confused. Will they serve us tea inside the car? But there's no table. Where would they keep all the biscuits and the cream and the sugar? What about the plates and cups?

Suresh suddenly appears at the window. He asks me to roll it down, then he hands two earthen cups with light orange liquid to my parents. I wait for the snacks, but none appear. I guess tea in India isn't exactly the same as tea in London.

My parents look at each other uncomfort-
ably but drink the tea anyway. It takes a bit
of effort because they usually take their tea
without milk or sugar. The Indian tea, my mom
whispers to me through gritted teeth, is nothing
but milk and sugar.

When Suresh asks how the tea is, my parents manage to praise it, which pleases him.
When they are done, Suresh takes the earthen
cups and crushes them underfoot.

5

By noon the heat is sweltering. All four of us are drenched with sweat. Suresh cranks up the air conditioning and continues jabbering to my dad. Then, all of a sudden, he announces that we've entered the city.

It looks no different than the little town or village where Mom and Dad had their first taste of Indian tea. There are stalls and carts and vendors with baskets. Some even have fish in them. Then I see some weird vehicles with three wheels—two at the back and one in the front. Suresh tells me it is called an auto-rickshaw.

I turn my head away, feeling bored, when all of a sudden I notice something colorful from the corner of my eye. When I look out the window again, I'm amazed.

Bright floral patterns, tribal art, and natural scenery adorn the city walls. The patterns change every four walls or so. The walls look new and neat and pretty, but I can tell the buildings are old. I must say that it is better than the graffiti that disfigures some of the walls in London. I can tell that this is the first thing my parents and I like in this new city.

Suresh tells us the art was part of a government initiative to beautify the city and make it poster free. He says that artists and college students helped paint the walls. There are hundreds of painted walls. My heart warms at the sight of all the colors. I love art, and I feel an urge to take out my paints and brushes.

Maybe Vijayawada is not a bad place after all.

6

By the time we reach our new residence, the sun is high and my spirits are low. Compared to the heat here, the summer in London is basically winter. Maybe Vijayawada is worse than I thought! I mean, how do these people survive in such deadly heat?

My t-shirt clings to my back because of the sweat. My handkerchief is soaking wet, and the sweat from my brow keeps coming and coming.

My usually calm mother also looks restless. My father has rolled up his sleeves. He seems to be itching at the nape of his neck. We are almost dying for some air, but there's none.

Suresh, who is unaffected by the heat, is busy unloading the luggage with the help of a security guard. After he's done, he points to a five-story building before us and says that we'll be on the fourth floor.

The building is a pale yellow color. It looks rather old. But who am I to complain when it's free accommodation in a new country? And, to be honest, all I want at this point is an air conditioner and an ice cream.

7

We're finally inside our new house. It has two bedrooms, a big living room, and a little dining area attached to the kitchen. There's air conditioning in one of the bedrooms. The three of us immediately go into that room and collapse on the bed. None of us says a thing.

The heat is horrid, the house is musty, the air conditioner leaks, and the area surrounding our apartment is dingy. We're all regretting coming here, but we don't say it. What choice did we have anyway? It was either come here or stay unemployed. Having been without a job for nearly a year, my father had to pounce on this opportunity—for our sake.

Now I realize that this move is difficult for my parents too, who have lived in London all their lives. We don't really have any living relatives, but all my parents' friends are back in London.

As for me, I have almost no emotional baggage. I've never been good with words or people. My voice just sticks in my throat when someone, especially a potential friend, talks to me. Because of this irrational shyness, I drifted towards books and art.

So my parents, my paints, and my books have always been my only friends. This move should be easy because all those things are here with me. I shouldn't act difficult. I need to be strong for my parents. I need to make this easier for them.

"What a lovely place, Dad," I whisper.

Dad, who's standing below the AC and cooling himself off, looks at me.

"I'm glad we came here," I lie. Although I had no friends back home, I loved the city. I loved living there. I loved our little home.

A tear escapes my eyes.

Dad comes to me and says, "Thank you, Erin, for trying to be strong. You don't have to pretend to like something you don't. I don't like this place one bit. But I'm going to stay strong and work hard. I'll get us out of this place soon, honey."

8

It's been a week since we first arrived, and it's been really hard. First of all, we had to go out to eat the first day because there was nothing at home. We searched online and found a Mc-Donald's in the city. Since Dad doesn't have an Indian driver's license yet, we have to depend on Suresh or public transportation. We'd had enough of Suresh for the day, and we were not up for public buses. So we went down the street to look for a cab.

The moment we stepped onto a bigger street, a cab appeared out of nowhere. The driver asked us to get in. Within minutes we were at McDonald's. My father paid the fare (which we later discovered was outrageously high), and we strolled into the fast food joint.

It was full of teenagers. And they were all staring at us. Probably because there are no blondes in India. My family and I are all fair skinned and blonde. It made Mom and me very uncomfortable.

In India, everyone stares at us. We are getting used to it now. Plus, the attention has been good in some ways. For instance, the other people in our apartment were eager to get to meet us. They brought sweets, some spicy trail mixes, and fruit to our apartment.

The auntie (I am now used to calling her that) who lives above us has been helpful. She and Mom have become good friends. She had been to London once, so we can talk about it with her.

She has taught us a lot so far, like how to get vegetables at the right price. Every morning a lady comes to the building with a cart of fresh vegetables. All the ladies either come to the cart or throw down a basket attached to a rope out of their windows. They haggle and bargain over the rates and ask for free curry leaves and coriander.

Since Mom can't speak Telugu (the lan-

guage they speak here), the auntie from the
fifth floor gets whatever vegetables we want. A
lady comes twice a week with fish, prawns, and
crabs in a basket.

As for meat, Dad has to get it from a butcher shop two streets away.

Auntie Vidya from the fifth floor invited us
for dinner several times. She is a bit younger
than Mom. She lives with her husband, Rao.

He calls my parents his brother and sister.
He calls me his niece. Although they are just
as excited as Suresh, I like them. I know they
mean well. And Mom and Dad are grateful for
their help.

Today they are coming to our apartment
for dinner. Mom made her signature fish and
chips and chocolate pudding. There is no oven
or microwave, but she still managed to make
amazing dishes.

Vidya and Rao enjoy the food and praise
my mom's cooking. Then Dad and Uncle sit
and talk about their jobs. Dad is a branch
manager in a multinational company. Uncle is a
journalist for an English newspaper. That must
be why his English is so good.

Mom and Auntie are housewives. They both
love cooking. They also love tea time, even
though their ideas of what goes with tea differs.

Mom prefers sweets and cakes, but Auntie likes savory fries, fritters, and crisps. The two ladies and two men are interested in learning more about each other. I have no partner to talk to, so I stick with my phone.

Minutes later, I hear Rao say, "Since you'll be staying here for a long time, shouldn't you enroll your daughter in a good school? There are a couple of great schools in Vijayawada."

"I thought it's summer vacation," Dad says.

"Yes, it is so hot here. I can't imagine that kids can leave their house in such heat," Mom says.

Vidya laughs. "Oh, *akka*, no!" *Akka* means "big sister" in Telugu. "It's June. The summer is almost over. This heat is nothing compared to the heat in May," she says.

I'm glad that we didn't come here in May.

"Schools have already reopened, *anna*," Rao says to Dad. *Anna* means "big brother" in Telugu.

"Already?" Dad is surprised.

"Of course," Uncle says. "But they will still accept students. Would you like to send your daughter to an all-girls school or a co-ed?"

My parents look at me. I choose the all-girls school. I know people are going to stare at me wherever I go. I think I'll be less uncomfortable around girls.

"Excellent choice, my dear," Auntie says. "I would have suggested the same. I know the principal of a wonderful girls' convent school. I studied there myself. Whenever you're ready, I'll take you there myself. I'll make sure you are admitted."

"Oh, Vidya. You are too helpful. Thank you so much," Mom says with her best smile.

"Oh, it's nothing, really," Auntie says. Her smile is even bigger than Mom's.

"Look at the time," Uncle says. "It's late. We better get going. I have work early tomorrow morning. It's been a wonderful evening. I don't know how to thank you enough."

"Yes. I hope you come for dinner at our place soon," Auntie chimes in. "But it's time to go to bed now."

"Not for me," Mom says. "I've got to do the dishes."

"You do the dishes yourself, *akka*?" Auntie asks incredulously.

"Of course. Don't you?" Mom is confused.

"No. Of course not! We have a maid for that," Auntie replies.

I'm surprised. Auntie and Uncle don't look

wealthy enough to have a maid. Mom and Dad seem to be thinking the same thing.

"Washing the dishes and clothes, sweeping and mopping the house every day... that is a lot of work. I find it a burden. That's why we have a maid. She's really more valuable than a diamond to me." Auntie laughs. "I can get you one. My own maid, Ratna, can come to your house after she's done with mine."

"No. We're just settling down here. And the maid would be an extra expense," Mom says slowly.

"Oh no! They work for very cheap. Mine does all the housework for three thousand rupees!"

"That is quite cheap," Dad says. "It's only about 33 pounds."

"Why don't you come to my house tomorrow morning? You can see if you like her work," Auntie says.

Mom accepts the invitation. After thanking us again, our guests finally depart.

9

I'm now the student of a convent school. It's called Rowan School for Girls. There are girls of all ages and sizes here. It has many grades and sections. After lower kindergarten and upper kindergarten, there are classes from one to twelve. Each class has five sections from A to E. I have been admitted into the E section of seventh standard. Today is my first day of school.

The uniform has a dark blue shirt and a white skirt that goes halfway down my calves. I have to wear black knee-length socks and white ballerina shoes. There's no makeup, no nail polish, no tattoos or henna, no mobile phones, and no jewelry except earrings and a watch. I have to part my hair into two braids and use white ribbons. I'm thankful that my hair is only shoulder length. If it were longer, I would have to tie it into ugly upturned braids.

I look at myself in the mirror after spending an hour getting ready. I think I look horrible. Mom, of course, thinks I look "*sooooo cute.*" She kisses me on the forehead then hands me a lunch bag and a bottle of water.

The school is far from our apartment, but my parents signed up for the school bus. At 8:10 AM, I hear an impatient honk. I hug Mom and Dad and run outside. I show the bus driver my bus ID card to enter.

The moment I step onto the bus, all eyes land on me. Even the driver stares at me before telling me to have a seat. I want to stand in the front and say, "Hi! I'm Erin," but I've never been good with words or crowds. I lower my head and walk to a seat near the back.

A soft murmur fills the bus. I know all the girls are talking about me. Some are staring, but I had already prepared for that so it doesn't faze me. Still, I become unsettled when the murmurs and stares seem to increase with every new passenger that boards the bus. I try my best to ignore it.

The bus picks up four girls after me. The fifth stop is the school. As we exit the bus, I hear a loud bell chime. All the girls run to the front of the school, so I follow them. There, three or four thousand girls stand in neat rows facing a huge stage.

Eight tiny girls stand on the stage with a mic in front of them. A bald man with a key-board sits in one corner of the stage. It looks like a badly arranged choir concert. There was nothing like this back at my London school. For some reason, it frightens me.

I jump when someone taps my shoulder. It's a short, plump lady. She wears a sari just like Auntie Vidya.

"What are you doing here?" she barks. "Get in the line."

Her accent makes even English sound like Telugu. She repeats her order, but I can't understand a thing. I can see that she's getting irritated, but I don't know what to do. I'm suddenly overwhelmed. My eyes well up. The lady's voice is so harsh and loud that a few girls look in my direction.

It doesn't help that I get shy in front of people. My face reddens with embarrassment, and my legs start shaking. My teary eyes threaten to give way like a dam. And then I hear a sweet voice behind me.

"She's in my class, miss. I'll take her to the line."

I turn and see a tall, dark, thin girl. She has the biggest eyes I've ever seen. Her hair is long and black. Even though she has tied her braids up, her hair reaches the end of her spine. She has a smile that seems to melt the howling lady.

"Doesn't this girl know how to answer for herself?" the lady asks. "Is she wearing make-up? She is so pale. Makeup is against school rules."

"Sorry, miss. She's new and very shy," the girl says sweetly. "She's not from here. She's a foreigner. That's why her hair is golden and her face is white."

The lady grunts. "Fine, take her to the line. The assembly is about to start. Sister will be on stage soon."

"Okay, miss," the girl says. She instructs me to follow her. We take one step before the girl suddenly stops and turns. Then she says in her sweetest voice yet, "Sorry, I forgot to wish you good morning, miss."

The howling lady practically melts to water now. She smiles. "Good morning, Vennela."

Vennela nudges me. I muster a smile. I also wish the lady a good morning. She accepts my greeting and tells us to be on our way.

Vennela leads me to a line of girls. Some girls turn and wave at Vennela. They all get a smile in return.

A sudden hush falls over the school. I hear a booming voice over the speakers. "Begin," it says.

I look up and see the principal of the school. I had seen her only for a second when I had come for admission. Now I can observe all her features clearly. She's a plump nun in a gray dress that falls to her calves. She's wearing stockings and stylish strappy sandals with a small heel. She has almost completely white hair, and her face has a permanent frown. I instantly dislike her.

On her command, music starts playing. The girls on the stage and all the girls on the ground begin singing. Then, one by one, the girls on stage read a moral story. They finish by giving us a "thought to remember." All of this is followed by the school anthem, which is sung with such patriotism you'd think it was a national event.

Finally, one of the girls says a common prayer and then the principal grimly tells everyone to go to class.

The ground shakes as all the rows of girls start moving in various directions. I start panicking and looking around. There's a tap on my shoulder again—it's Vennela.

"Sorry for bringing you here to my class line like that. Miss Suseela is short-tempered. I didn't want her to spoil your day." She says all this in perfect English.

"Thanks a lot," I say.

She flashes her dazzling smile again. "No problem. So you're new, right? Do you know which class and section you are starting?"

"Seventh class, E section," I say.

Vennela's face lights up. "That's my class!"

10

I actually look forward to school these days. For the first time I have someone to talk to at school. Vennela is amazing. Since the first day of school, she hasn't left my side. She helps me in every class. She even let me borrow her notes from classes I had missed because of my late admission.

That first day was very hectic. Every teacher asked me to introduce myself. They all wanted me to tell the class a few things about London. The class of fifty girls would stare at me expectantly. But not a word would come out of me. I would just stand there with my head lowered, shaking.

This happened in all the eight periods. And in every class, Vennela came to my rescue. She told the teachers that I was not comfortable speaking in front of everyone since it was my first day. All the teachers listened to her. They instructed her to help me with my work.

"It's because I'm the class representative," Vennela told me later. "I'm expected to help everyone."

"Seems like a tough job," I say. I'm surprised that I find it easy to speak with her.

"Oh, but I like it," she says cheerfully.

Vennela is the exact opposite of me. She's popular among the students *and* teachers. She's talkative, and she's active. The only similarity is that we both like to study. But she's much smarter than me. It's as though she's naturally smart. I, on the other hand, have to work really hard. I'm not naturally intelligent. But since I'd turned to books because of my shyness, I was labeled a nerd back in London.

Here, however, nerds seem to rule the school. Only the girls who study and score the highest in every test have the confidence to strut around like a beauty queen. They have the favor of all the teachers, but there are many jealous students. Vennela has managed to

impress both the groups. And I can see why—
she's kind and helpful. There's practically no
flaw in her character. Even if there were a flaw,
her engaging smile and big brown eyes would
probably make you ignore it.

Mom and Dad were thrilled to hear about
my first real friend. They told me to invite her
over for tea. But Vennela said no because she
had a lot of work to do at home.

I wonder what work a twelve-year-old could
have on a Sunday.

11

I can't believe I'm saying this, but I'm actually glad that I came to India—to Vijayawada especially.

Because here, in just a month, I've found something I never had hope of having back in London—a best friend!

Back in London, people avoided me, and I avoided them. People thought I was happy that way. *I* thought I was happy that way. But deep down, I knew that I was miserable. Every time I saw a group of friends, I longed to have friends too. How wonderful it would be to have a friend my age so we could face the world together!

It's not like I didn't try to make friends. One time, with a lot of courage and effort, I made up my mind to speak with some of my classmates. But when I approached them, they looked at me as though I was a crow trying to be a peacock. You know what I mean?

There's a story we were taught in Hindi class yesterday. It was about a crow who was star struck by the beautiful peacocks. He wanted to be friends with them. So he changed himself. He got fake feathers. Then he ridiculed his fellow crows for being plain and ugly. His fellow crows abandoned him out of disgust. And when the crow approached the peacocks, they rejected the crow for being a wannabe. In the end, the crow was alone and friendless.

I'm not a crow. But my classmates in London thought I was a crow. They expected me to play the part. If I tried to be anything but a crow, they'd look at me funny.

The night before my first day at Rowan, I decided I would make a fresh start. Shy or not, I had decided to do something, anything, to make friends.

And this is exactly why I'm glad to have come to India. I didn't even have to try to find friendship—friendship found me!

Vennela is talkative enough for the both of us. She asks a lot of questions and says a lot of things—mostly about school and studies. We have Hindi and Telugu classes because one is the national language and the other is the state language. Since I know nothing but English, Vennela has taken it upon herself to help me pass these classes.

Once, I asked her, "Why do you always help me? Even that first day in school, you helped me although you didn't know me. Why?"

"I just felt like it," she said. "For some reason, when I saw you, I felt like being your friend. That morning you were so lost and scared. My first day of school, I, too, had a horrible start. I just didn't want someone else to suffer the way I did. I did what I hoped someone would have done for me."

She looked at me with serious eyes for a moment. Then she smiled. "For some reason, Erin, I felt that you would do the same for me. I felt that you would help me if I was in a pinch."

I frowned. "I don't think so. I mean, I would help you, but not the way you did. I'm not really good with people and words. I could never do what you did. I don't think I'll be able to speak for you in front of an entire class or even a teacher."

"That's what you think. But if you care about something or someone enough, you can do wonders. That's what I read in a self-help book yesterday," she said proudly.

It didn't make sense to me, but I nodded. We continued chatting about different things. Still, her words stuck in my mind—if I really cared about something, would it really make me do something wonderful? First of all, do I care about anything very much? I thought I cared very much about staying in London. But that didn't make me perform any "wonder" to stop us from moving. Maybe I didn't care much about London anyway.

I won't lie, I would want to perform a wonder—but how would I do that? And what do I care about?

Ah! All this philosophy makes my head hurt.

12

I thought Vennela was named after vanilla ice cream. But she said that her name means "moonlight." How cool is that? And it suits her gentle nature.

I have no idea what "Erin" means. I only know that Dad and Mom combined their names (Eric and Mirrin) to make mine. I think it's a beautiful gesture, but I want my name to reflect who I am.

For now, my name shows that I'm partly like Dad and partly like Mom. But nothing can be further from the truth in terms of personality.

I'm not charming and talkative like Dad,

and I'm definitely not a pillar of strength like my mom. I do look like them, but I would have liked to have their personality traits more than their features.

Actually, I think there is one quality that my parents and I share—a quality we have developed recently—the *ability to adjust.*

Vijayawada doesn't have most of the facilities we had in London, like a water heater, an oven, or a microwave. In London we weren't stared at when we went outside. Unlike London, Vijayawada doesn't have restaurants that are open late, on holidays, or on Sundays.

At first we complained about all these things. But now we don't mind. It's so hot here that a water heater isn't needed. On the rare days when it's a bit cold, Mom heats up water on the stove. Mom says that she has become a creative chef because there's no oven.

Now she can make even cakes and cookies on the stove! And without a microwave, we all get fresh meals since we can't reheat leftovers.

We are all used to being stared at now. Sometimes, it's fun.

Some people actually want to take a photo with us. It feels like we're famous. To some degree, it has made me less shy in front of

crowds. Sometimes, when the staring gets uncomfortable, we stare right back at them until
they turn away. I think I've become braver by
all these experiences.

For some odd reason, the malls (there are
three or four huge malls here) and most of the
shops shut down by nine or ten at night. It's
very inconvenient, but we manage. If we want
to go somewhere, we just go early and come
back early. Now we sleep early too.

As for the six-day work and school week,
Dad and I have come to value the free time we
get on Sundays. So a Sunday is never wasted.
We either go out and have fun, or we stay at
home and do something creative. I paint, Mom
experiments with new dishes, and Dad helps
Mom in the kitchen.

We are actually happy here. Mom, especially, says that she's more relaxed than she ever
was in London. And do you know the reason?
Ratna, the maid!

Mom hired Ratna two months ago. She's
the same one who cleans Auntie Vidya's
house. My mom was unsure about hiring a
maid, but now she says that she'd choose a
maid over any other luxury. Because Ratna
takes care of all the cleaning and washing,

Mom has more time on her hands. She's so pleased with the maid that she regularly gives the maid a few extra rupees as a tip.

The maid seems very happy. She works harder and harder every day. She's as friendly as all the other Indians we've met. She's slim but strong. She's always smiling and has big brown eyes. And she calls my mother *amma garu*, which means "mistress." (I've been learning a lot in my Telugu class.)

"*Amma garu*," Ratna says one day.

"*Enti?*"—*What is it?*—Mom asks. Auntie Vidya has been teaching Mom Telugu. Now she knows how to ask people's names, introduce herself, ask for the price of food, and say "thanks" and "goodbye."

Ratna says something in Telugu that we can't understand. We take her to Vidya, who translates for us.

The maid was asking if she could bring her daughter to work next Sunday. Even though the maid worked at three houses, she needed more money. Apparently, her daughter would be married off soon. So, they needed to save money for her wedding. Besides, her daughter needed to learn how to be a maid, since she would probably work as a maid after marriage.

Mom tells Ratna to bring her daughter as often as possible.

She promises to give Ratna more than the extra hundred rupees she asked for so that Ratna's daughter can have a nice wedding. Ratna sheds tears of happiness.

13

Back in London, I had tried to get good grades.

I studied hard, but I was too shy to raise my hand in class. But here, speaking to Vennela has given me practice. I've actually started raising my hand when a teacher asks a question. Often only Vennela's hand and mine shoot up into the air. But we rarely get called on to answer because the teachers like to target those who don't study.

I'm excited about school today. First period is a political science elective course. For some reason, I find politics very interesting. We didn't really have this subject in my London school. It helps me know more about India as a country.

Rowan has this awesome system where we can pick two additional elective courses to study along with our regular subjects. I chose the Fine Arts course and the Indian Constitution course.

I am on the way to class when I see Vennela standing just outside the door. She's lost in her thoughts. Even though some students push past her, she doesn't seem to notice. I call her name, but she doesn't respond.

I go up to her and tap her shoulder. She jumps and looks at me. Her eyes are red and swollen.

I can tell that she has been crying.

"Vennela, what's wrong?" I ask.

"Oh, it's nothing, nothing," she says hurriedly and heads inside the classroom. She doesn't go for the first bench as she usually does. Today, she sits in the back. I follow her and sit beside her.

"Something's wrong. Tell me what happened," I say.

She shakes her head. "Everything's fine, really."

"Vennela, I—"

All the students suddenly stand up and say, "Good morning, sir."

The teacher has entered the class. He asks everyone to sit down and begins his lesson. He is very strict, so I decide to talk to Vennela after class. Besides, she seems to be listening to the lesson. I sigh and focus on the lesson too.

Today we learn about child labor and child marriage in India. I know what child labor is, but I don't really know about child marriage.

The teacher explains how in India, lots of children are forced to work because of poverty. And most of the children work in dangerous mines and factories, or even in houses as maids.

He talks about the kids in India who die due to bad work conditions. I cringe when I hear that some children start working when they are as young as five. I'm 12 and I hardly work. Even at home, especially since we've hired a maid, there's no work at all. I don't even have to clean my room!

We learn there's an act in the constitution that seeks to stop child labor so that children can live safer, better lives. It's the duty of every Indian citizen to educate their children. But since it's not a law, it's not really followed.

Then the topic shifts to child marriages. In India, some people marry off their children at a young age. There have been cases of five-year-old girls being married! I'm horrified. I try to imagine getting married now, at age 12, and a chill runs up my spine. Even the thought of leaving my parents for an unknown person (marriages in India are mostly arranged) is mind-numbing. And in India, marriage comes with many new responsibilities for the bride.

Thankfully, child marriages are banned in India. The girl has to be at least 18 years old, and the boy has to be at least 21 to be married. I'm glad the laws are strict about this. I whisper the same to Vennela, but she's staring off into space. I whisper her name, but she doesn't hear me.

I see a tear run down her right cheek. I whisper her name again, worried now.

"Who's talking?" the teacher asks. I stop whispering.

Next we learn about the laws in the constitution that are against child marriage. He tells us about some non-government organizations that stand against child marriage, and he gives us the helpline to which we can report child marriages. The teacher tells us that complaints can be sent to the police office for child marriage cases. The emergency number is 1-0-0.

I take it all down in my notes. The bell rings and before I can ask Vennela what's wrong, she runs out of the class.

14

I see Vennela in third and fourth period, but I don't get a chance to speak with her. I decide not to trouble her during class. We sit together for lunch anyway.

Vennela sits with me at lunch but hardly eats. She often brings very little food, and she's usually starving by lunch time. I don't think the amount of food she brings can fill anybody's stomach. Usually I share my food with her. Today she doesn't touch her food. I want to ask her what's wrong, but I keep quiet because she looks so miserable.

Lunch proceeds in silence. Just before it

ends, she says, "I'm sorry, Erin. I'm not in a good mood today."

"I understand. I'm here if you ever feel like talking about it," I offer.

It looks like she's about to say something, but then she changes her mind. She shakes her head and says, "Nah, it's okay. I'm fine. Thank you."

Nothing exciting happens the rest of the week at home or at school. All teachers start revising their lessons because the midterm exams start in two weeks. But I'm not able to concentrate because Vennela looks more miserable every day. When she sees me, she tries to smile and act normal, but it doesn't work. She has stopped eating and she hardly speaks. There was a surprise test in Chemistry yesterday. She submitted an unanswered test for the first time.

Today's Sunday. I usually wake up late, but I hardly slept last night. I'm unable to put Vennela out of my mind.

I find my mom engrossed in a newspaper. I say, "Mom, Vennela was upset and spaced out the whole week. It worries me."

Mom smiles. "I'm glad you found a friend, Erin." I smile. Mom continues. "Maybe something happened at home. Maybe her parents scolded her. It's not uncommon here. I've seen many of our neighbors scold their children for things like schoolwork."

I shake my head. "Vennela's an A student. She always gets the highest marks in every subject. I don't think the parents of such a kid would be angry..."

"But there are different kinds of parents. Some are soft, and some are strict. Some are not pleased, no matter what their child does." Mom sighs. "I hope Vennela's parents aren't like that."

"Oh no, they're not like that. They're... they're..."

"What?"

"I actually don't know what kind of parents they are, Mom. And I don't remember her saying anything about them. That's strange. She talks about all sorts of things usually, but I don't think she has ever told me about her family."

"That is odd. Maybe she doesn't like talking about it. Or maybe she just forgot."

"C'mon, Mom. Who forgets their family?"

Mom doesn't answer. I keep talking. "The whole week was horrible because Vennela hardly talked or ate. And she flunked a test."

Mom's immersed in the newspaper and doesn't respond.

"Mom?"

No response.

"Mom!" I say loudly.

She jumps and asks. "What?"

"What are you reading?"

"An article Mr. Rao from the fifth floor suggested. It talks about child marriages in Andhra Pradesh," Mom says.

I'm surprised. "We learned about child marriages in school this week. I didn't know they occurred in this state too."

"Yeah. It sounds horrifying. Some parents force their kids to marry old people for money. The poor kid has to shoulder a lot of responsibilities after marriage."

The doorbell rings and my mother goes to answer it. I take the newspaper and read the article.

CHILD MARRIAGE STILL A REALITY
(Vijayawada, Andhra Pradesh)
Even though child marriage has been banned in India for several years, child marriages still exist. The results of a recent survey have rocked state authorities. Andhra Pradesh

is among the top three states where child mar-riages are prevalent. Children who are teenaged or younger are being forced to marry adults and old relatives.

These shocking incidents occur mostly among the illiterate, the economically backward, and the highly conventional rural people who believe that a girl child is a burden.

Inequality is the root of this issue. Since girls are sometimes considered pariahs, outcasts, or nonpersons, money is not spent on their education. Many people still believe that girls shouldn't be educated.

This is sad. In almost every examination, girls have been outperforming boys in academia, according to a survey by a private organization.

"Darling, can you please get my purse from the bedroom?" Mom asks from the front door.

The article is far from over, but I decide to read it later. I get Mom's purse from her room and go to the front door.

"Thanks, dear. Ratna has brought her daughter with her today. But I forgot that we're all out of floor cleaner. I'm giving her the mon-ey to get some from the store down the street," Mom explains.

"Okay," I say, turning to go back to the newspaper.

"Wait, Erin, won't you say hello to the Ratna's daughter?"

I hear a small gasp from the door when mom says my name. I turn to see who it is.

I am shocked by who I see in the doorway.

15

Vidya and Ratna stand together by the door, but there's someone behind them. I see a girl who's thin and tall and dark. She's dressed in a dirty, multicolored sari. Her hands are shaking, and her large brown eyes stare at me in horror.

It's Vennela!

Before I can react, Ratna says something in rapid Telugu. Even though I'm able to understand Telugu much better now, Ratna's words don't register. I can't take my eyes off Vennela, who stares at the ground.

"She's saying that it's her daughter—the one she told you about," I hear Vidya say.

"Oh! The one that's going to be married?" Mom asks.

"Yes. She's here to learn housework and earn a little extra to save up for her wedding." Vidya is even more chipper than usual. "She just finished dusting my house. She works slow, but she'll learn. At least she's a neat worker. I gave her a large tip."

Mom smiles and invites them inside. She asks them to sit down. Vidya finds a chair, and Ratna sits on the floor. Vennela is about to sit on a chair but Ratna clears her throat angrily and gives her a stern look. Vennela flushes red and sits down on the floor.

I'm speechless. I don't know how to process the scene before me.

So Vennela is the maid's daughter? And she's here to work? But she's only twelve. And— and— I gasp. *She is about to get married soon?!*

"Oh, I forgot about the floor cleaner. Vidya, can you please tell the maid to get some." Mom takes out some money.

The maid listens to Vidya, takes the cash, and hurriedly walks out the door. Vennela is sitting alone on the floor with her head lowered.

I want to talk to her, but I can't get the words out of my mouth.

"What's your name, dear?" Mom asks.

Before Vidya can translate the question, my friend answers, "Vennela."

For a moment, nothing seems wrong. But then it hits them.

"Y-you know English?" Vidya is bewildered.

Vennela is flustered. She acts as though she didn't understand the question. She looks at me pleadingly, asking for help.

But I'm angry. Why didn't she tell me the truth?

"She does," I almost yell.

"What?" Vidya is still in shock.

"She knows how to speak English. She's Vennela, the best student in school," I say angrily. My eyes are welling up with tears.

"And she was my friend. Or so I thought," I say slowly before I storm to my room.

A bony hand grabs my wrist. I turn back to see Vennela with red eyes and tears streaming down her face.

"I'm sorry, Erin," she whispers.

I immediately feel horrible for lashing out, but I don't know what to say.

"I'm sorry I didn't tell you about my family. I thought—"

"You thought I wouldn't be friends with you if I knew you were a maid's daughter? Do you think I'm that shallow?"

ERIN AND THE INDIAN BRIDE

Her eyes widen. "No, no, no... I know you're not shallow. You're the best person I know."

"Then why didn't you tell me?"

"Because I thought I didn't deserve to have a friend like you. I'm just a petty maid's daughter... I don't have the right to have such nice friends. I hid the truth so that I could feel worthy of being your friend." She sinks to the floor and cries softly.

I kneel down and hug her. "I always wondered if I was worthy of having a friend like you... You're the only friend I've got." I cry too.

"Sorry, Erin. I'll never hide anything from you ever again. I know now that you'll always understand."

16

I explain everything to mom and Vidya right away. Vennela requests that we act as though we've seen her for the first time. Her mom already hates that she is studying at school.

Ratna views English education as something against her tradition and values. She thinks that girls who are taught more than required will become morally bad. She only allowed it because it was free since Vennela got some scholarship. Sending Vennela to school would allow Ratna to do her work in peace.

At home, Vennela acts as though she has learnt nothing from school, not even English.

If her mom finds out that she knows educated people who might support her education and oppose her work and marriage, Vennela would never be allowed out of her house again.

Vennela's mom enters. We all fall silent. Ratna takes Vennela to the kitchen and shows her how to do the dishes. Later they sweep and mop the floor.

My mom tries to control her tears. Even Vidya remains unusually silent.

Just before leaving, Vennela mouths a "thank you" to me. My mom gives her a lot of money. The maid leaves our house in high spirits, while Vennela sadly drags her feet.

Just as we shut the door, Mom bursts into many questions. But I can't answer her because I had no idea about Vennela's plight.

"I didn't know she was so young," Vidya says sadly. "I would never have let her work for me if I knew."

A realization dawns on me. "It's child labor, isn't it?" I know the answer, but I still ask. "She's a victim of child labor, isn't she?" My voice is shaky.

Mom lowers her head and takes a deep breath, but Vidya nods. "I'm afraid she'll soon be a victim of child marriage, too."

17

I spend a sleepless night thinking about Vennela. I can't get the image of her in a dirty sari out of my head. By the time I fall asleep, it's four in the morning. Within minutes I wake up due to a nightmare about Vennela's marriage.

It's 7:30 AM. I get ready for school even though I'm tired and sleepy. I need to see my friend.

I can't find her in the assembly line. I ask some of my classmates, but none of them know where she is. My stomach drops when I think of the possibility of Vennela being pulled out of school.

After assembly, I run to my first class. Relief washes over me when I see her sitting quietly in one of the last benches in class. I call out her name and she looks up. Her eyes are red and swollen again. I can make out the red shadow of a hand mark on her left cheek.

Without thinking, I grab her hand and pull her up. She is shivering and has a fever. I tell one of the other girls that I'm taking Vennela to the sick room, and I rush out of the classroom with her.

The sick room is empty, thankfully. I don't bother to find a nurse because I know Vennela would be uncomfortable explaining the mark on her face. I make her lie down on a bed and I sit beside her.

"Thank you," she mutters.

I've never seen her like this. She is always so confident and full of life. She loves studying, but I'm pretty sure she can't stand to be in class at the moment.

"Get some rest," I say. My voice still shakes because I cannot believe how different Vennela looks. She seems to have aged and weakened.

Is she really going to get married? Will she leave school?

"My mother will take me out of school, you

know..." she says weakly, as though she has read my mind.

"I know." I don't know what else I can say.

"She's going to take me to her village, Per-akalapadu, in three days. Some old coot is waiting to marry me there." She is so angry and frustrated now that she sounds like she's growling.

"Why is your mother giving you away to an old man?"

"She never thought of me as her own. She thinks that girls should be married at a young age and that they shouldn't be too smart. She thinks having a girl is a curse because girls eventually become someone else's property. To my mother, a girl's not worth her money or time."

She takes a deep breath. "I feel like cursing her, Erin, but I can't. I know that those beliefs don't belong to her. She, too, was married at a young age. She was younger than me. And ev-erything she knows was taught to her by other child brides in the village.

"It's a miracle that she allowed me to go to school. One of her employers coaxed her to send me here. They even helped me get the scholarship. My father was angry about it, but he agreed because I get a monthly stipend as part of the scholarship."

"Maybe if you showed them how great you are doing here—" I begin, but she cuts me short.

"It's not going to work, Erin. Yesterday I asked them to let me take my exams before marrying. This was their reply." She points to the red hand on her cheek. "Besides, ever since I was told that I'd be married off, my brain has stopped working. I can hardly under-stand anything that's happening around me." She bursts into tears. "I am terrified."

I can't bear it. Every time I look at her, I imagine her in an Indian bride's outfit with shackles on her hands and feet. It's a frighten-ing and mind-numbing thought.

"Run away," I blurt out.

She is taken aback. Her eyes widen and she stares at the floor. After a second, she chuckles.

"I'm serious, Vennela," I say.

She stares at me. Her eyes are like fire. "Tell me, Erin, if you were in my place, what would *you* do?"

My heart starts pounding. I'd imagined myself in Vennela's place countless times last night. And every single time I felt utterly help-less and broken.

"Tell me," her voice is half mocking and half angry.

I can't get the words out of my mouth. I'm ashamed because I know I would do nothing. I could do nothing. I feel helpless and useless.

"I know exactly what you would do—*nothing*. You would be too scared to speak against your parents or go against their word. You would do whatever was asked of you," Vennela says bitterly.

I cringe because I know it's true.

She continues speaking, but now her tone is softer. "I will do the same, Erin. I can't help it. You can't help it. The crazy thing is, I always knew this day would come. But I had some wild, stupid hope that education would save me from following my mother's footsteps in life. How stupid I was. Just a stupid village girl from some stupid village."

She stares at the roof as though she wants it to crumble and fall on her. Then she whis-pers, "Go away, Erin. There's nothing we can do. We're hopeless."

I quietly get up and start to leave. I wait in vain for her to stop me. My throat burns from crying and my head reels from lack of sleep. But I can't go home before lunch anyway, so I go to my third period class—the elective on the Indian Constitution.

18

"Erin?"

I feel someone nudge my elbow.

"Erin!"

The teacher's loud voice makes me jump and I stand.

"Are you daydreaming? I asked you a question. What is child marriage? Do you know the answer or not?"

"Child marriage is when minors are married," I answer slowly. I'm used to answering in class now and don't feel shy or intimidated.

"Yes, and what is the minimum age required for legal marriage in India?"

"18 for girls, and 21 for boys," I reply.

"Good. Now, if a child in your neighborhood is being forced to marry, how can you stop it?"

He has revised this question multiple times in class because it will be on the midterm examination. I know the answer perfectly by now.

"I can call the appropriate authorities to stop the wedding."

"Who are these authorities and how will you contact them?"

"They are the police, who can be contacted by dialing 1-0-0. I can also use the child helpline, which is 1-0-9-8."

I gasp. *I've got the answer to my problem!*

There is thunderous applause from everyone in class. They are hushed by the teacher. "Very good, Erin. You may sit down now. I thought you weren't paying attention in class. Seems like I was wrong. Now, class, next we'll revise..."

I stop listening. Suddenly, I don't feel helpless or shy in the face of a problem. For once, I know exactly what to do, and I'm not afraid to do it.

19

Riiiing Riiiiing Riiiiiing Riiiing

I wipe the sweat from my brow and clutch my phone. I'm sitting in my room, and I've just dialed the police emergency number. After four rings, someone picks up.

"Hello?"

I hurriedly cut the call and throw my phone on the bed. My hands are trembling. I was never good with words or people. I know that I have improved, but that's just in school. Can I really speak to a stranger? To a police officer? What if they don't believe me? What if they want me to speak in Telugu? What if... what if...

I shake my head. I should not give up at a time like this. Surely the police understand English. If not, I can ask Vidya for help. The police sound scary, but they're here to help.

I grab my phone and dial 1-0-0 again. I still can't find the courage to speak to a police officer. But this is something I need to do.

I take a deep breath and hit the green button. Someone answers the phone on the fourth ring.

Before they can say anything, I burst out, "Please help, sir. This is a really serious matter." I almost cry into the phone. "My friend Vennela is being forced to marry someone. She's only twelve. And she's such a good student, and a good friend. If she gets married, it'll destroy her." I can't help but cry now.

"Please, calm down, child." The man's voice is soft. "Please give us more details. We will do everything we can to save your friend. I'll ask you some questions, okay?"

"O-okay."

"What is your name and your age? And where are you from?"

"I'm Erin Vainwright. I'm twelve, and I'm from Vijayawada."

"Okay, Erin, now tell me about this friend of yours," the policeman says.

"My friend's name is Vennela. Sorry, I don't know her full name. But she studies at my school and she's in the same class as me."

"Which class, and which school?"

"Seventh class at the Rowan School for Girls."

"Okay. So Vennela is twelve years old, right?"

"That's right. And her mom, who works as a maid at my house, is forcing Vennela to marry an old man in another village. That village's name is Pera...Perakal....um...."

"Perakalapadu?"

"Yes, that's it."

"Okay, and what is the maid's name?"

"Ratna."

"Okay. Does this maid still work at your house?"

"Yes. She has finished her work for the day, but she'll come tomorrow and the day after, too. After that she is taking a leave because that's the day of the wedding. Can you stop it? Can you stop the wedding?"

"Yes, my dear. Three days will be enough time. We can help your friend." I can feel the police officer smile.

"Thank you so much," I say, relieved.

"Is there something else?"

"No... Wait! Yes, there is something else."

"Yes?"

"Vennela is a really great student. Can you make sure that she is allowed to continue her education? She really wants to study, but her parents don't want to send her to school. Can you do something about that?"

There's a small pause before the officer answers. "Yes, we can. Thank you for bringing it to our notice—"

"Wait, there's something else too. I'm sorry..." I say uncertainly.

"No problem, dear. What is it?"

"Umm, I hope you will not send Vennela's parents to jail. I know they are bad for forcing their daughter to marry, but they are all Vennela has. I'm sure she loves her parents. She would not be happy without them. Ratna is good natured. Her mindset is just a bit wrong."

"Since the wedding hasn't occurred yet, we won't be arresting your friend's parents. We'll simply go and counsel them, explain to them how harmful child marriages can be and why they're illegal. We will also show them how important education is, especially for a girl. You don't need to worry about your friend or her parents."

I'm not totally convinced. "Does counseling really work?"

"Don't worry. The police can be very persuasive." He chuckles, "Besides, professional counselors will take care of the job."

I feel relieved. "That sounds good."

"Now please give me your address."

I give my details to the police officer and thank him for helping me.

Before cutting the call off, he says, "Thank you for being a vigilant citizen and a responsible friend. You should be proud of yourself. It takes a lot of courage to do what you did today. You sure are a brave girl."

20

I want to skip school today because I'm expecting the police to come to my home to speak to Ratna. But mom and dad send me to school anyway.

Last night, when I told them I had called the police, they were shocked. At first, they didn't say anything. Then they said that I should have told them before calling.

I apologized, but I'm not really sorry. I know that my parents would have been just as scared to call the police. I would never be able to forgive myself if I had acted too late.

My parents promised to deal with the police

and assist them in every possible way. They promised not to speak about it to Ratna so she wouldn't run away before the police came.

I'm sitting in first period Mathematics class. Vennela is absent today. At first I was afraid that her mom might have taken her to the village early. But then I put that thought out of my head and tried to think positively. Mom always said positive thoughts are helpful. I finally decided that Vennela must have stayed back because of the fever she had.

The day is unbearably long. I'm very anxious about the police. Will they come today? Or will they forget? No, I'm sure they'll come.

By the end of the day, I have played out a hundred different scenarios in my mind. Some of them are good, but most of them are dreadful. Still, I wasn't expecting the scene that greets me when I finally arrive at home.

There's no one in the house except my mom, who's busy making tea. It's just like any other weekday. Nothing seems out of the ordinary. I doubt whether anyone had even been to our home the whole day.

I head straight to the kitchen and say anxiously, "Hi, Mom. Did the police come?"

Guessing by how calm she looks, I'm thinking the answer is no. But to my surprise, she says they did.

"Really? What did they say?" My hands start shaking and I start sweating.

"Nothing."

"Wh-what?" I can't believe my ears. "How can that be?"

Mom shrugs. "Two policemen came around 10:15 and they took Ratna away. That's all. They said nothing. They just asked her name, and her daughter's name. Then they took her away."

I spend another sleepless night thinking of all sorts of things that the police might have done to Vennela's mom. Did they really counsel her? Or did they throw her in jail? And what about Vennela's dad? What about Vennela?

The next day, I rush to school, but Vennela's absent again. This fills me with dread. My brain starts imagining all sorts of things. Things that I'm afraid to even talk about. My head starts reeling, and I drag myself to the sick room. I climb into an empty bed and sleep the rest of the day.

Just before the last bell, I wake up from a nightmare. I'm sweating all over and my head hurts badly. I try to shut my mind off as I hurry to the school bus.

I've never had tea, but today I decide to

have one. Dad always drinks tea to relieve his headache. Maybe it will help me too.

The bus drops me in front of my house. I stumble once or twice while walking up the apartment building. I remember that I had not had lunch. That must be why I feel weak right now. My mind's out of control. I can't stop thinking about Vennela. I'm in such a daze that even my vision is blurred.

When I see Vennela at my door, I think my mind is playing a trick. I shake my head, but the dream-like sight of my friend doesn't go away.

Suddenly, I feel bony arms around my neck. I hear soft sniffles in my ear. I come back to my senses when I hear that familiar sweet voice, "Thank you, Erin..."

Vennela!

I snap out of my daze and look at my friend. She steps back and smiles. She is shaking and crying, but she has a wide smile on her face, "Thank you so much! I cannot thank you enough!"

My parents, Rao, Vidya, and a police officer come and stand by the door. Vennela continues thanking me.

I blush and feel a bit shy. "Oh, c'mon, it's

no big deal..."

"No big deal? Are you kidding, Erin? It's a very big deal for me!" Vennela cries. "Because of you, I don't have to get married. Because of you I get to live a free life..." She holds my shoulders. "Because of you, I get to study."

My eyes widen. "What? Are you serious?"

She wipes her tears and nods. "The police counseled my parents. Now they both agreed to let me go to school. And I don't have to work or marry until I'm ready."

I squeal and hug her tightly. I don't think I've ever been so happy in my life.

"I'm sorry that I called you hopeless, Erin. I should never have told you that you could do nothing," Vennela says softly. "I'm not a good judge of people."

"No, you are a good judge of people. Remember you told me that you thought I would help you too someday?"

"Yes, and you doubted yourself then too." She laughs.

"Yes, but now I know how right you were," I say.

"Me?"

"Yes. You said that if you care about something or someone enough, you can do wonders." I smile.

Vennela's smile broadens, too. But she suddenly stops smiling and she looks nervous.

"What's wrong?" I ask her. Now I'm getting scared, too.

She stares at me for a long time. The suspense is nerve-wracking.

"I just remembered that we have exams next week and I was absent for two whole days. I missed a lot of revision! I really need a wonder now."

My parents and the other adults look at each other and burst out laughing. I can't help giggling too. Vennela still looks anxious though. So I grab her hand and lead her to my study table.

"C'mon, you can borrow my notes. We can study together."

About the Author

Javeria Kausar is an Indian author and poet who wants to spread awareness about neglected issues through her works. She has been published in the 2017 Scythe Prize Anthology and the Sweek Microfiction book for her flash fiction. She has also been awarded the Damodarshree National Award for Academic Excellence for her essay in 2017. In 2018, she won the 2018 Haiku contest by Wordweavers India.

She is currently pursuing her master's degree in English. She dreams of helping humanity and making a difference through her words.

About the Publisher

Storyshares is a publisher focused on supporting the millions of teens and adults who struggle with reading by creating a new shelf in the library specifically for them. The ever-growing collection features content that is compelling and culturally relevant for teens and adults, yet still readable at a range of lower reading levels.

Storyshares generates content by engaging deeply with writers, bringing together a community to create this new kind of book. With more intriguing and approachable stories to choose from, the teens and adults who have fallen behind are improving their skills and beginning to discover the joy of reading.
For more information, visit storyshares.org.

Easy to Read. Hard to Put Down.

www.ingramcontent.com/pod-product-compliance
Lightning Source LLC
Chambersburg PA
CBHW051310170626
46809CB00004B/1829